AF585537

How to Be a

Juliette MacIver & Carla Martell

SCHOLASTIC
SYDNEY AUCKLAND NEW YORK TORONTO LONDON MEXICO CITY
NEW DELHI HONG KONG BUENOS AIRES PUERTO RICO

For Heliana and Olivia,
who also know how to be cats ~ J.M.

For Nathan and Alex, who would love
a duckling and a kitten with equal affection ~ C.M.

This story is reflected in a real-life, furry-feathered friendship!
Watch Animal Planet's *A Momma Cat and Her Yellow, Feathered Kittens* on YouTube.

First published in 2024 by Scholastic New Zealand Limited
Private Bag 94407, Botany, Auckland 2163, New Zealand

Scholastic Australia Pty Limited
PO Box 579, Gosford, NSW 2250, Australia

ISBN 978-1-77543-887-8

A catalogue record for this book is available from the National Library of New Zealand.

---

12 11 10 9 8 7 6 5 4 3 2 1 4 5 6 7 8 9 / 2

Illustrations created using pencil, watercolour, pen and ink, and digitally composed

Publishing team: Lynette Evans, Penny Scown and Abby Haverkamp
Designer: Vida Kelly
Typeset in Shaking Three
Printed in China by RR Donnelley

Scholastic New Zealand's policy is to use papers that are renewable
and made efficiently from wood grown in responsibly managed forests,
so as to minimise its environmental footprint.

Sque-e-eak!
Read this
Best Picture Book
WINNER too!

Three small cats
begin to mew.

Two go

and Duck does, too.

"Come," says Mama,
"Time to chat.
I'll show you how
to be a cat."

"This is how
we wash our fur.
Mama will show you.
Eyes on her."

"Lick your paws,
now rub them through."

The cats all wash . . .

and Duck does, too.

"This is how
we climb a tree.
Use your claws
and follow me!"

Up they go!
They're quick and true.
They reach the top . . .

and Duck does, too.

"This is how,
with flair and flounce,
we chase our prey.

We stalk . . .

wait . . .

POUNCE!

The kittens stalk.

They wait on cue,
and then they
POUNCE!

And Duck does, too.

"Now use your teeth
to tear and chew."

The cats all eat . . .

and Duck does, too.

"Now off you go."

They're all so keen!
They climb. They stalk.
And pounce. And clean.

Then . . .

Three big cats come.
"Look at that!
This duck believes
that it's a cat!"

The big cats laugh.
"What's wrong with you?"

The kittens hiss . . .

and Duck does, too.

Back home to Mama
the kittens race.
But Duck hangs back
all out of place.

"Am I a cat?"
Duck feels so small.
"Do I belong with you
at all?"

"Don't listen, love,
to what they claim.
Not all cats
are made the same.

Duck, you have the skills
down pat.
You know just how
to be a cat."

So snuggling up
in Mama's fur,
they curl up tight . . .

and Duck goes

PURR.